It's Good to Have a GRANDPA

Maryann Macdonald

illustrated by
Priscilla Burris

Albert Whitman & Company
Chicago, Illinois

In memory of George, a loving grandpa—MM

For Russel, Avery, Cruz, Eliseo, Omer, Ruben,
and all you awesome grandpas out there—PB

Library of Congress Cataloging-in-Publication data is on file with the publisher.

Text copyright © 2019 Maryann Macdonald
Illustrations copyright © 2019 Priscilla Burris
First published in the United States of America in 2019 by Albert Whitman & Company
ISBN 978-0-8075-3675-9 (hardcover)
ISBN 978-0-8075-3674-2 (ebook)

Printed in China

10 9 8 7 6 5 4 3 2 1 WKT 24 23 22 21 20 19

Design by Aphee Messer

For more information about Albert Whitman & Company,
visit our website at www.albertwhitman.com

100 Years of Albert Whitman & Company
Celebrate with us in 2019!

It's good to have a grandpa,
because grandpas like to have fun.

If you help your grandpa rake up a great big pile of leaves, he won't mind if you jump in them.

He'll never say, "What a mess!" or "Now we have to start all over again."

Not Grandpa!

He lets you cover him in leaves.

He'll cover you too.

He might even give you a ride
in his wheelbarrow.

My grandpa helps me search for skinks.

We like to look at roly-poly bugs too.

Grandpa always has a magnifying glass handy.

"You never know when you'll need one of these," Grandpa says.

Grandpas don't mind if you comb their hair to look like a woodpecker.

They are good at being silly.

"What happened to your hair, Grandpa?"

"It went to Honolulu with my teeth."

"No!"

*"Yes! One morning I woke up and they were both gone.
They liked Hawaii so much they never came back."*

Grandpa and I walk to the bakery together.

He always gets the same kind of doughnut.

I always get a different one.

We like to play cards together too.

Sometimes I win. Sometimes he wins.

Grandpas can forget things.

They forget it's Friday.

They forget where their glasses are.

But they never forget story time.

We both climb into Grandpa's chair.

It's big enough for two.

Then Grandpa tells me what happened
to him a long time ago,

when he was a surfer

or a soldier

or a hippie.

Some of Grandpa's
stories are even true.

Grandpas like to take you with them when they go places:

the library,

the pancake house,

the beach.

They teach you things too.

How to hammer.

How to float on your back.

How to dance.

Grandpas don't get tired of playing catch.

They don't get tired of building skyscrapers or garages, either.

Sometimes they let you beat them at tic-tac-toe.

If your grandpa lives far away, you have to go visit him.

Are we there yet?

Are we there yet?

Maybe you have to fly in an airplane.

When you finally do get there, you are both *so* happy!

But if your grandpa lives on the next block, you are happy too.

He can pick you up from school.

You can have a milkshake on the way home.

He can help you with your homework.

If you can count all the change in his pants pocket,
he might give it to you.

You can be happy almost anywhere
with a grandpa.

Take your grandpa to the playground.

Let him see you hang by your knees
from the monkey bars.

Show him how you climb up the slide backwards and go down face first.

Play tag.

Let Grandpa try to catch you.

Play hide-and-seek.

Let him try to find you.

Not all grandpas are the same, of course.

Some like to play airplane.

Some like to play chess.

Some like to do puzzles.

Some like to go bowling.

Some take you for rides in their pickup.

Some take you for rides in their convertible.

But all grandpas know how to have fun...

especially mine!